First published in the United States, Great Britain, Canada, Australia, and
New Zealand in 2019 by NorthSouth Books Inc., an imprint of NordSüd Verlag AG,
CH-8050 Zürich, Switzerland.

Distributed in the United States by NorthSouth Books Inc., New York 10016.
Library of Congress Cataloging-in-Publication Data is available.
ISBN: 978-0-7358-4342-4
Printed in Latvia 2018
1 3 5 7 9 • 10 8 6 4 2
www.northsouth.com

Mr. Squirrel
and the King of the Forest

by **Sebastian Meschenmoser**

North South

"The King of the Forest appears in many forms," said the billy goat. "He can have the head of a fox and the ears of a hare. His head is crowned with leaves, and the morning star shines in his heart."

"He comes out of the mist only once in a hundred years,

and then he wanders through the fields and forests."

"He brings us spring.

Wherever he goes, the plants turn green and the flowers blossom."

"Whatever the king says is the truth and is the law.

He brings order to all things and teaches us how to lead a better life."

For a long time Mr. Squirrel kept dreaming about the King of the Forest. Would the king also come to his forest one day and teach him to lead a better life?

One morning Mr. Squirrel woke up because something was stinging his nose. It was a smell. And it was the sort of smell he knew very well.

But who could be so rude as to leave it right outside his front door?

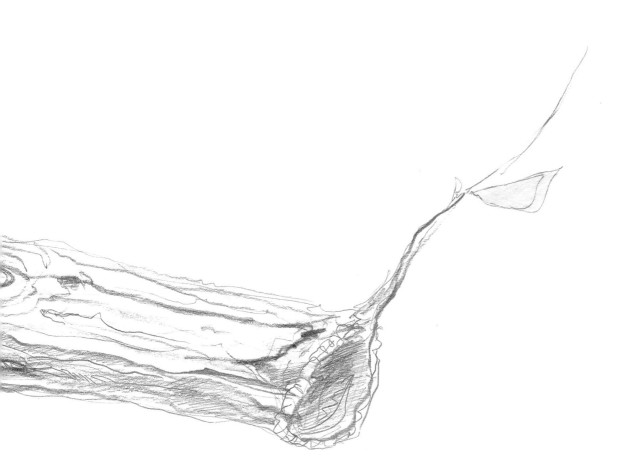

He looked out, and what he saw was a creature with the head of a fox! His ears hung down loosely like those of an old hare. He had the spotted skin of a cow and the short legs of a hedgehog.

Mr. Squirrel also saw antlers with green leaves,
and from the creature's breast shone a sparkling
morning star.

It could only mean one thing.

The King of the Forest had come!

What luck and what an honor to meet the king himself!

Would he teach Mr. Squirrel to lead a better life?

He had already brought spring,

and now he had good advice to give to all the animals.

In order to lead a happy life, they must dig lots of holes.

They must run around in circles until they felt giddy.

They must frequently scratch behind their ears.

And they mustn't forget to sit and stare.

But the most important thing of all was that they must leave their scent wherever they lived.

Then everything would be exactly as it ought to be.

So saying, the king left. He had told them all he knew, and now it was time for his lunch.

Mr. Squirrel had already dug lots of holes, run around in circles, and given his ears lots of scratches. All he had to do now was to leave his scent where he lived.

Unfortunately, however, at that moment Mr. Squirrel couldn't manage to go.

Luckily, Mr. Squirrel's friend the hedgehog lived
in the same tree.

News about the new rule spread
very quickly through the forest.
But what would happen if someone
else wanted to move into your tree?

In fact, the hedgehog had already left
his scent somewhere else that morning.
But he didn't want to live there.

They decided to go to the lake and have a good drink.

Even that was far from easy.

Because everybody was following the wise advice
of the king . . .

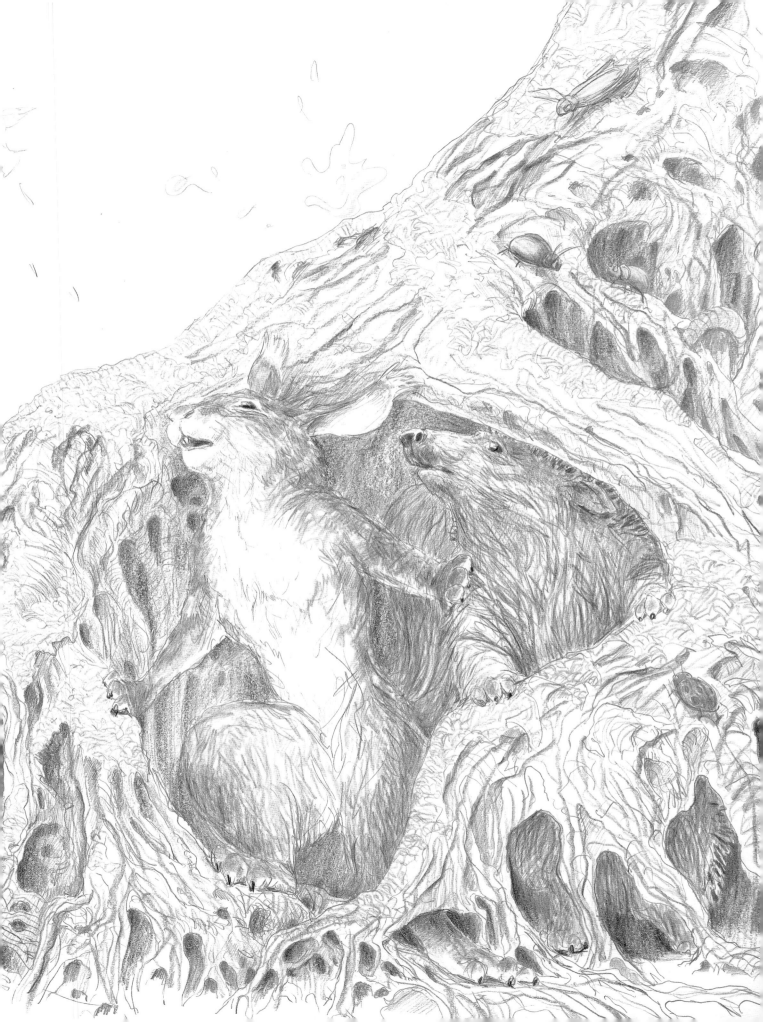

There was no place where somebody
didn't want to live. . . .

The bear was at home wherever he went—that was clear.

But now that everyone had left their scent on their home, nobody wanted to go back there again. The whole forest stank to high heaven!

Mr. Squirrel wanted to get some advice from the King of the Forest, but it seems he had disappeared again for the next hundred years.

They couldn't wait that long.

There was, however, one place where nobody lived yet
and where the wisdom of the king was still unknown.

It was a very small place, but all the same there was enough air to breathe.
Among so many friends, the hundred years were sure to pass quickly.
Then the king would return, and all would be well again.

A strange creature seemed to be walking through the mist.
Some animals thought they could see the head of a fox, and
others saw the ears of a hare.

Quite a few believed they'd seen a big stag.

When the first rays of the sun shone through, the creature faded away and disappeared.

The air was cool, and there was no smell except that of fresh grass.
Mr. Squirrel knew for sure that this was his home.

Even if the true king never came back, life was now as beautiful as it could ever be.